CASEY JONES

by
Carol Beach York

illustrated by
Bert Dodson

Folk Tales of America

Troll Associates

PROLOGUE

Among all the heroes in American history, Casey Jones has a very special place. Unlike some folk heroes, who were half real and half tall tale, Casey Jones truly existed.

Casey was a railroad man. He loved trains, everything about them. There was never anything he wanted more than to be an engineer on the railroad.

Today, young people may dream of going to other planets in a spaceship. But when Casey Jones was growing up, being an engineer on a railroad locomotive was the biggest and best you could wish for.

Casey did become an engineer. And he proved himself a brave man as well.

In railroad talk today, "Casey Jones" means an engineer—especially a fast one!

Library of Congress # 79-66313
ISBN 0-89375-298-3/0-89375-297-5 (pb)

10   9   8   7   6   5   4   3

Casey Jones was born in Cayce, Kentucky. He got his nickname from the town. The words aren't spelled the same, but they sound the same.

Casey's real name was John Luther Jones. He was born in 1864, at the tail end of the Civil War.

There were railroads in America by then. But they were skimpy. Most goods still traveled by boat. Towns were built along rivers, so people would be nearby the boats that brought them flour and tea, bolts of cloth, barrels of molasses. And all the other things they needed.

But after the Civil War, the railroads began to grow. *And grow.* AND GROW.

They spread out everywhere across the land—even to the far-off West, where there were still roaming buffalo and a life that was mighty wild.

As the miles of track stretched out here-there-and-everywhere, things changed. Towns sprang up along the tracks. They no longer had to stay huddled along the riverbanks. Goods came on freight trains that chugged across the countryside, puffing steam and tooting whistles. Sometimes the train had to stop and clear a cow off the tracks. Then it chugged on again.

Nothing would be so grand as to be an engineer.

Casey used to sit in the hayloft and pretend it was the cab of a big, shiny engine. He waved to the barnyard animals just to get into practice for being an engineer.

"Where are you, boy?" his father would call, and Casey would have to stop being an engineer and throw feed to the chickens.

The railroads had their problems as they grew. Tracks got washed out in heavy storms. There were wrecks on weak bridges. Fires started from the stoves that were used to heat the cars. Train robbers hopped aboard, waving guns and stealing everyone's money.

"Land sakes," Casey's mother said. "I don't know why you'd want to work for the railroad." She didn't think it was a very safe job.

But as Casey grew old enough to work for the railroad, things improved some. An air brake was invented that was far better than the old-style brake. And train robberies were less frequent—after Jesse James got shot.

"Railroads are getting safer all the time," Casey told his mother.

"Hmph," she said. She wasn't so sure about that. But she could see there was no holding Casey back.

Of course, Casey couldn't start right off being an engineer. Engineer was the *top* of the list! He had to start out doing odd jobs and running errands at the roundhouse, where the locomotives went for repairs. Casey probably ran a couple hundred miles of errands at the roundhouse every day. But he loved being around the locomotives. Someday he was going to have one of his very own.

After being a roundhouse worker, the next step was fireman on a freight train.

A fireman had a hard job in those days. He rode in the cab with the engineer, and Casey liked *that* part. But that was the only good part. A fireman had to shovel coal under the boiler to keep up steam as the train rushed along. If there wasn't enough coal to keep the boiler

water hot and steam coming out, the train couldn't make time. And making time was important. Trains were supposed to be where they were supposed to be—at the right time. The fireman had to keep hard at work every minute. It was backbreaking, sweaty work. But a good fireman, sooner or later, was bound to become an engineer.

The early passenger trains were not at all comfortable, but people rode them from town to town, jolting on hard wooden benches, munching out of box lunches, and warming their hands at potbellied stoves. Conductors came through, punching tickets. Babies cried.

Some train rides were short, some were long. Pioneers going out to the new land in the West traveled by train. Everything was changing.

Cayce, Kentucky, was a small town. Women wore sunbonnets when they went to the general store. Children rode horses bareback along the dusty roads. Not much happened in Cayce, and the train station was about the most important spot in town. Certainly it was the most exciting. Children stood by the tracks to wave to the engineer when a train came through.

"Here she comes!" Casey liked to scramble up on the low station roof to be the first to spot a train.

"Git down off of there," the stationmaster scolded. But Casey wasn't listening. He was waving at the engineer. And the engineer was waving back.

16

When the train had gone, the children would begin to drift away, and Casey would slide down to the ground.

"About time," the stationmaster grumbled.

"I'm going to be an engineer someday," Casey said.

"Me too," the others shouted. But most of them grew up to be bank clerks and farmers and schoolteachers and traveling salesmen. That was all right for them. As for Casey Jones, he never wanted to be anything but a railroad man.

"If you don't break all your bones on the roof first," the stationmaster warned. "You better get on home now and do your chores."

And Casey did have chores to do. His father was a farmer. There were eggs to gather, cows to milk, fields to hoe. But Casey never stopped dreaming about trains, about being an engineer someday.

Nothing beat the sight of the great "iron horse" puffing up the track with a cloud of steam overhead.

Nothing was as beautiful as the sound of a train whistle in the night.

Casey Jones was just twenty-six years old when he got his first locomotive. He was young for an engineer. Even so, it had taken him ten years of hard work.

He was well known and well liked by the other railroad workers on the Illinois Central Line. They clustered in the train yard to slap his back and shake his hand when they heard he was going to be an engineer.

"Bring her in on time, Casey!"

"That's what I aim to do," Casey answered the roundhouse workers, switchmen, and brakemen, gathered around in their overalls and heavy work boots.

"You've got to get yourself a whistle, Casey," the yard foreman reminded him.

"I'm getting the best there is!" Casey hollered back. His face was bright with excitement. He'd been waiting a long time for this day.

It was the custom for engineers to buy their own train whistles, and Casey got himself a fancy one for sure. It had six pipes, and it wasn't long before everybody who lived along Casey's route knew the sound of that whistle. Children, farmers, store clerks, and house-wives always knew when Casey Jones' train came through town.

Besides his whistle, Casey was known for speed. He always got his train in on time, like he said he would. Soon he got the Canton to

Memphis "Fast Mail" run. That was Canton, Mississippi, to Memphis, Tennessee. And it *was* a fast mail run with Casey Jones in the cab.

His locomotive was Number 382, and he took care of it with pride. He saw to it that the soot was cleaned off the boiler after every trip. The brass was polished. The paint was always fresh. Everything was sparkling clean.

"Shucks, Casey," his fireman, Sim Webb, joked, "you can eat off the cab floor."

And that was just about true.

Casey whizzed along through the countryside, his hand on a wide-open throttle most times. He waved to the barefoot boys so much like himself once upon a time. He pulled on his six-pipe whistle till the hills echoed. Sim Webb shoveled in the coal, and Number 382 ate up the track.

From his high seat, Casey could see the land for miles around, and he always felt good when he was in that cab. It was where he had always wanted to be. If there were bad weather or bad track ahead, Casey kept right on full speed and brought his train in on time.

The weather and the tracks were both bad on the night of April 28, 1900. Rain poured down. The tracks were gleaming, and the heavy rain blurred the road ahead. The countryside was lost in darkness. It was 188 miles from Canton to Memphis, and there were sharp curves and uphill stretches. It wasn't an easy trip even in good weather. Casey stared ahead into the driving rain and kept his hand steady on the throttle.

As morning came, the men in the Memphis train yard watched the storm and peered up the track into the gloom.

"Think he'll make it on time?" they asked each other.

"Casey always does," a switchman bragged. "A little rain won't slow him down."

But this was more than "a little rain." There might be track washed out. Rivers were rising high under the bridges. Lightning whipped through the air.

"Casey'll make it." The switchman chewed on his pipe and squinted up the track.

The other men shook their heads.

"He can't make it this time," they said. "Not in this weather."

It was beginning to get lighter, and a cheer went up as the men saw the faint beam of the 382's headlight in the distance.

"Here he comes!" The switchman threw his cap in the air. "Here he comes!"

Casey had made it into Memphis on time—
dog-tired and glad to climb down from the cab.

"A hard run, Casey?" a yardman called with
a wave of his hand.

"I've seen better." Casey laughed. He was a
tall, handsome man, but his face was drawn
with weariness. It had been a long night. His
fireman walked with him through the yard,
and railroad workers called and waved to them
as they went by.

"You did it, Casey!"

All Casey wanted right then was a good night's sleep. Tomorrow would be time enough to check the engine, see that the brass was polished, and the cab clean enough to "eat off the floor."

He shucked off his boots and fell asleep almost at once.

But Casey hadn't been asleep long when a messenger came. Rubbing the sleep out of his eyes, Casey listened to the excited messenger.

The engineer who was supposed to make the return trip to Canton was sick.

Casey pushed tired fingers through his rumpled hair.

He was already reaching for his boots before the messenger had time to ask, "Can you do it, Casey?"

"Get Sim," Casey said, striding to the door.

At the train yard Casey found the 382 with steam up, ready to roll.

"The rain's stopped at least," he joked to Sim Webb. Sim was already hard at work shoveling coal. He was proud to be Casey's fireman, but he sure was tired after the long, rainy trip the night before.

"We can always sleep tomorrow." Casey settled into the cab seat just as the yard foreman came running up.

"Casey!" the foreman yelled up to the cab. "You're already an hour and thirty-five minutes behind time."

Casey grinned down. He didn't feel so tired now. It always felt good to get back in the 382. He touched his fingers to his forehead in a salute to the foreman. *I'll make up the time,* the salute said.

The wheels began to turn. Casey and Sim were on their way, with a string of twelve mail and passenger cars behind.

The foreman ran along beside the engine. "Casey, there are two freights ahead—keep an eye out for them. They'll pull off on the siding at Vaughan."

Casey waved back. The 382 was rolling too fast now for the foreman to keep up. He fell back and stood watching as the long train of cars pulled away from him into the dark night. He could hear Casey's whistle as the 382 cleared a signal board, picking up speed already.

"Good luck!" the foreman called. But Casey was too far away to hear.

The 382 sped through the night. Wheels clicked over the ties. Steam bellowed out the smokestack. Sim poured on the coal, and Casey's whistle shrilled over the fields.

Fifty. Sixty. Seventy miles an hour.

At the town of Sardis, there was a stop for passengers. The 382 had already made up some time, and it was soon on its way again. Sweat poured down Sim's face. His muscular arms gleamed with sweat. His shirt stuck to his back. They were making up time, and they were making it up quickly.

Seventy. Eighty. Ninety miles an hour.

Telegraph poles loomed up in the darkness and flew past. The cars rattled from side to side. Wheels pounded over bridges and thumped over switches. There was clear track ahead.

At the next stop, Casey had made up more time.

Eighty. Ninety. One-hundred miles an hour.

As he neared Vaughan, he was almost on schedule.

"We'll do it, Sim!" Casey kept his hand on the wide-open throttle as they highballed along.

On the sidetrack ahead, the first freight had pulled off the main line. But as the second freight turned onto the siding, an air hose broke. The brakes locked. Two cars and the caboose were still on the main line.

Frantically, the train crew leaped from the cars to see what could be done.

"Get at it men!"

"Clear those brakes!"

Voices pierced the darkness. "Move her *out!*"

The men could already see the headlight of the 382 barreling toward them through the black night.

There wasn't time to fix the broken hose—

and the crewmen watched in horror as the
light grew closer.

A whistle blasted the silence.

"By heavens, it's Casey Jones!"

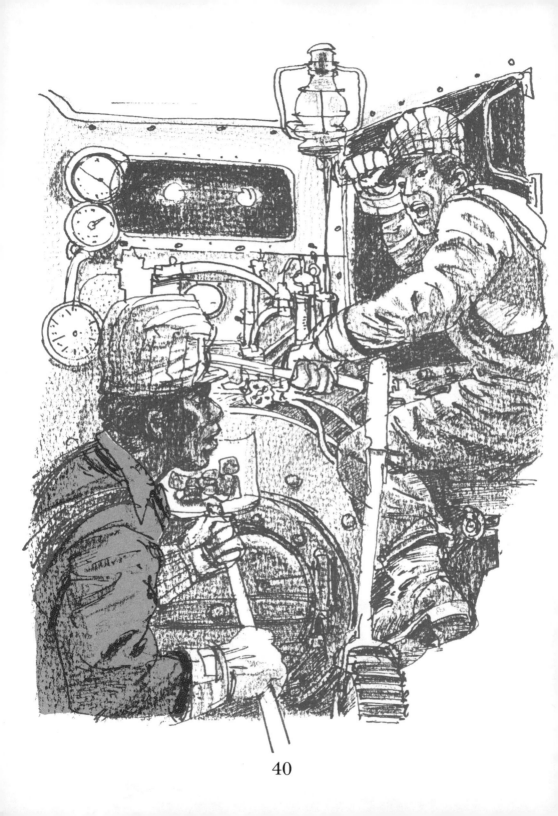

40

The headlight was getting closer. A crew-man seized an explosive—a warning torpedo—and raced down the track toward the onrushing train. He was numb with fear. He couldn't run fast enough! There wasn't even time for *this!* The train was too close. He knew that—but he ran as far toward the train as he could before he put the torpedo on the rails.

Just as the 382 rumbled over the torpedo—exploding it with a stupendous *boom*—Casey saw the red tail lanterns of the stalled train ahead.

Sim Webb saw the lights at the same time. "*Casey*—" The fire shovel clattered from his hands as he gazed, terror-struck.

Casey pulled the air brake—his whistle screamed—sparks flew from the grinding wheels.

"*Jump, Sim!*" he shouted. He was standing now, pulling the brake with every ounce of strength he had.

The taillights were rushing at them through the darkness. Hard ground was flashing by below the engine. Sim stared down at the ground and cast a desperate glance at Casey.

"Come on, Casey—"

But Casey held the brake. *"Jump, Sim!"* he ordered again, and as Sim jumped out into the dark, rushing night, the 382 tore into the rear of the freight with a deafening crash. Metal

and wood shot through the air. Steam roared
from the smashed boiler. The freight caboose
was shattered to bits, and the freight cars split
open and were hurled from the tracks with a
thunderous, crushing blast.

Within moments, lanterns dotted the darkness as the stunned freight-train crew rushed to the scene, expecting the worst. To their amazement, they found the passenger cars still on the track behind the mangled 382. Not one passenger had been killed.

Casey hadn't been able to stop the train completely. He knew he couldn't. But keeping

his hand on the brake had slowed the train enough to save all these lives. If he had jumped with Sim, the crash would have been much worse.

Sim Webb lay unconscious, but alive, on the ground where he had jumped.

Casey Jones was dead, a shred of whistle cord clutched in his hand.

The railroad men who knew Casey Jones had liked him well. They had lost a good friend. Not long after his death, a roundhouse worker named Wallace Saunders wrote a song in tribute to Casey. Casey had always had a cheerful word for him, and Wallace Saunders couldn't forget that.

People still sing the song today. And Casey Jones will never be forgotten.